Oh No, Gotta Go!

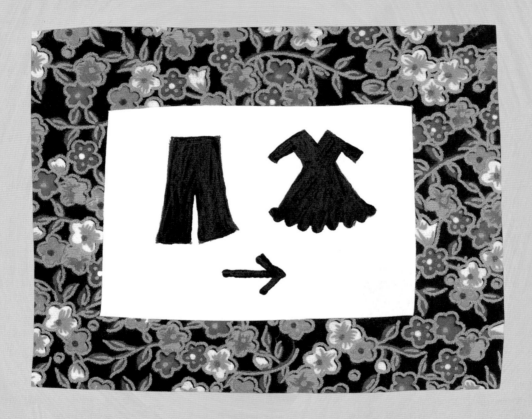

Susan Middleton Elya

illustrated by G. Brian Karas

G. P. PUTNAM'S SONS • NEW YORK

We were out driving, down the **camino**.
Papá and **Mamá** were dressed **muy fino**.

The backseat was mine, my favorite spot,

until I remembered the thing I forgot.

"Where is **un baño?**

¿Dónde está?

I really do need one," I told **mi mamá.**

Mis padres were talking, their voices down low.
"Didn't you ask her if she had to go?"

"No, didn't *you*?"
Dad's ears became red.
"I'm sorry—**lo siento**. I meant to," he said.

"I drank lots of juice,"
I said to **mi padre**.

"Don't worry; we'll find one,"
promised **mi madre**.

Papá checked the bakery—**la panadería**,
but it wasn't open because of the **día**.

"On Sunday, **domingo**, the sign says **cerrado**.
The baker is tired. He feels **muy cansado**.

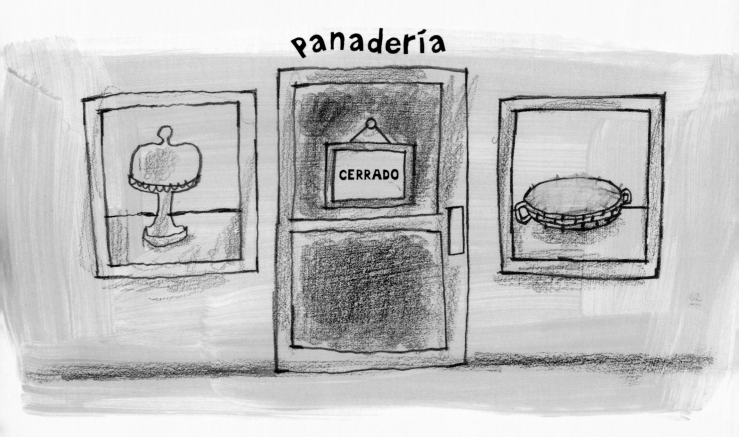

"No haircuts today at the **peluquería**;
no shoes will be sold at the **zapatería**.

"But we'll find a bathroom, and quickly—**de prisa**.
So sit back, relax, and enjoy the cool **brisa**!"

Papá saw a worker out pouring **cemento**.

He backed up to ask the big stranger—**extraño**,

"You go down the street,
turn left at the **banco**,

the one with the fountain, a white building—**blanco**.

"Go down two more blocks, past the little red school.

Then look for the restaurant, the blue one—**azul**."

So we turned at the bank with the fountain—**la fuente.**

"Hurry, **Papá.**
¡Más rápidamente!"

We drove down a side street with neatly built **casas**,
saw gardens with pumpkins—big orange **calabazas**.

We passed the **escuela** and school bell—**campana**,
so quiet today, so noisy **mañana**.

We pulled up, at last, to the blue **restaurante**,
the fanciest building of all—**elegante**!

"**Papá**, stop the **carro**! ¡**Mamá, por favor**!
¡**Abra la puerta**! Please open the door!"

We raced to the **baño** with no time to dine.
We rounded the corner and then saw . . .

the line!

Mamá grabbed my hand. **"Con permiso,"** she said.
"She really can't wait!"
So they said, "Go ahead."

I went to the **baño**, came out with a sigh,
and thanked the nice ladies who let me go by.

Some nodded, some smiled, some touched my **cabeza**.
Then Dad found a table. He called out: "**¡Sorpresa!**"

"Let's eat here," he said. "We'll order **comida**, and if you're thirsty, please choose a **bebida**."

The waiter served **sopa** and then **ensalada**, next chicken—fried **pollo**—and more **limonada**.

Finally, for **postre**, he brought us some **flan**,
but I was filled up from the special bread—**pan**.

We paid for our meal, got into the car,
drove down the **camino**, had not gone too far,

when I asked **mis padres**, **Papá** and **Mamá**,

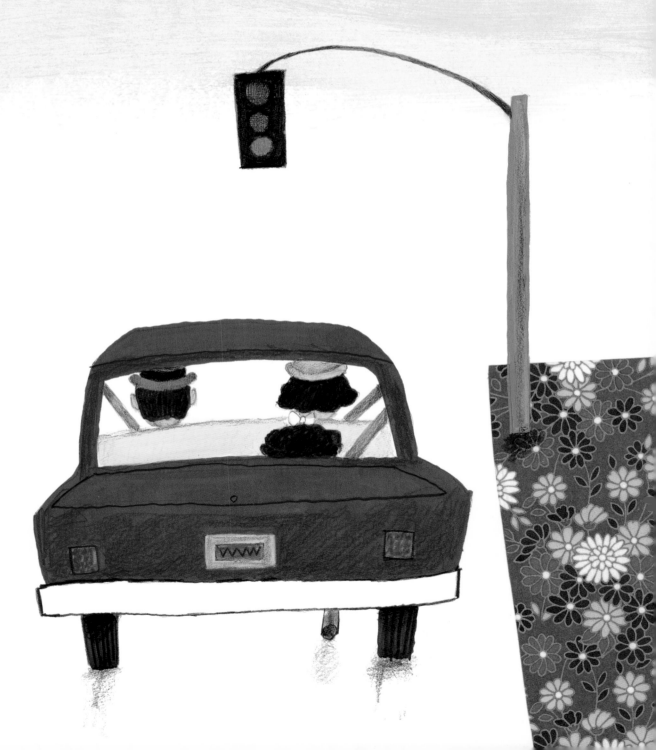

"Where is **un baño?**

¿**Dónde está?**"

Glossary and Pronunciation Guide

Abra la puerta (AH brah lah PWERH tah) open the door

Azul (ah SOOL) blue

Banco (BAHN koe) bank

Baño (BAH nyoe) bathroom

Bebida (beh BEE dah) drink

Blanco (BLAHN koe) white

Brisa (BREE sah) breeze

Cabeza (kah BEH sah) head

Calabazas (kah lah BAH sahs) pumpkins

Camino (kah MEE noe) road, highway

Campana (kahm PAH nah) bell

Cansado (kahn SAH doe) tired

Carro (KAH rroe) car

Casas (KAH sahs) houses

Cemento (seh MEHN toe) cement

Cerrado (seh RRAH doe) closed

Comida (koe MEE dah) food

Con permiso (KONE pehr MEE soe) excuse me

De prisa (DEH PREE sah) quickly

Día (DEE ah) day

Domingo (doe MEEN goe) Sunday

Dónde está (DOHN deh ehs TAH) where is it?

Elegante (eh leh GAHN teh) elegant

En este momento (EHN EHS teh moe MEHN toe) this very moment

Ensalada (ehn sah LAH dah) salad

Escuela (ehs KWEH lah) school

Extraño (ehs TRAH nyoe) stranger

Fino (FEE noe) fine

Flan (FLAHN) custard dessert

Fuente (FWEHN teh) fountain

La (LAH) the

Limonada (lee moe NAH dah) lemonade

Lo siento (LOE SYEHN toe) I'm sorry

Madre (MAH dreh) mother

Mamá (mah MAH) mom

Mañana (mah NYAH nah) tomorrow

Más rápidamente (MAHS rah pee dah MEHN teh) quicker

Mi (MEE) my

Mis padres (MEECE PAH drehs) my parents

Muy (MWEE) very

Padre (PAH dreh) father

Pan (PAHN) bread

Panadería (pah nah deh REE ah) bakery

Papá (pah PAH) dad

Peluquería (peh loo keh REE ah) barbershop, hairdresser's

Pollo (POE yoe) chicken

Por favor (por fah VOHR) please

Postre (POCE treh) dessert

Rápido (RRAH pee doe) fast, quick

Restaurante (rrehs tau RAHN teh) restaurant

Sopa (SOE pah) soup

Sorpresa (sohr PREH sah) surprise

Un (OON) a

Zapatería (sah pah teh REE ah) shoe store